my picnic adventure

(wheat & gluten-free!)

wheat free — allergyadventures.com — ® — A world of serious fun

gluten free — allergyadventures.com — ® — A world of serious fun

GW00809132

This book belongs to

....

Written & designed by Hailey Phillips
Illustrated by Ivana Zorn

Enjoy finding food that's safe to eat. Boffle and his friends
will show you how to stay safe and have lots of fun as you
find your way through the allergy adventure maze.

Copyright © Hailey Phillips, 2013 Copyright © Ivana Zorn, 2013
Published by Allergy Adventures Ltd. in 2013 **allergyadventures.com**

Proudly made in the UK   ISBN - 13: 978-1-909710-02-3

START ►

Are you ready to start a magical allergy adventure?

This is Boffle and he's allergic to wheat. Inside his lunchbox is magical wheat and gluten-free food.
If you're lucky, join him for lunch and I bet he'll love to show you too!

"I'm sooo hungry!!"

Boffle is so excited because it's lunchtime.
He knows that when he takes his first bite,
the food will take him to a magical place!

He finds a big comfortable seat,
opens his lunchbox and reaches inside...

...to find oodles and doodles
of stringy rice noodles!

"Tee-hee"

This pot of white squiggles,
Gives Boffle the giggles.

Chasing food around the pot,
To make a noodle knot!

Saucy carrots slip and slide,
And mushrooms try to hide.

So with a big cheeky grin,
His fork dives right in!

WhOOShhh

"I'm getting smaller!"

Boffle sucks the first noodle up!
"Here we go, hold on tight!" and he
magically shrinks into his lunchbox.

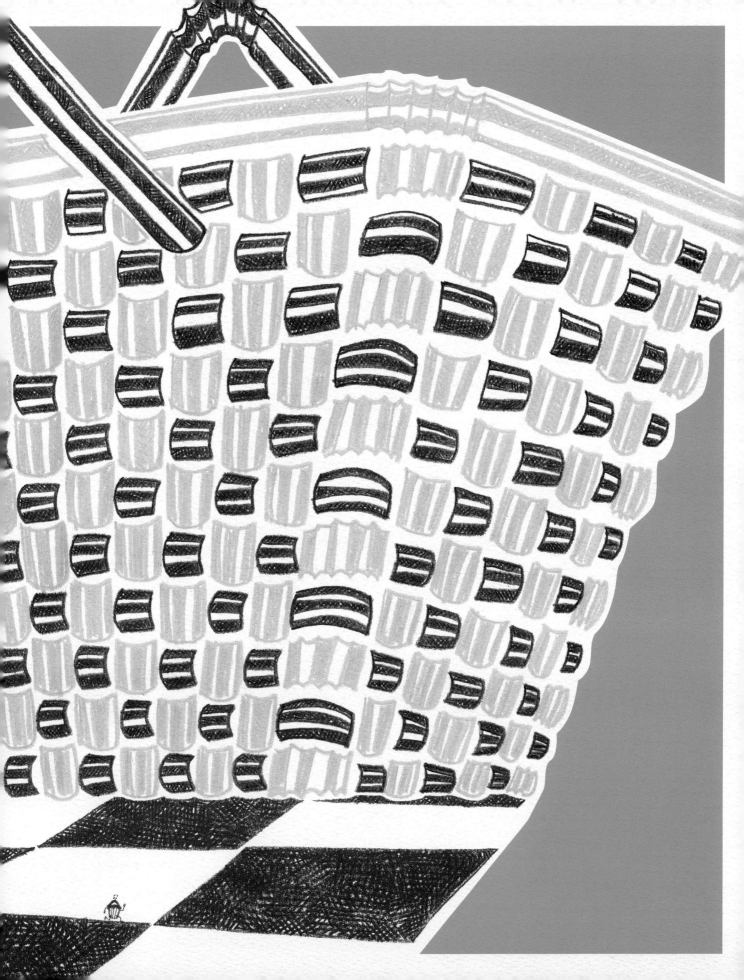

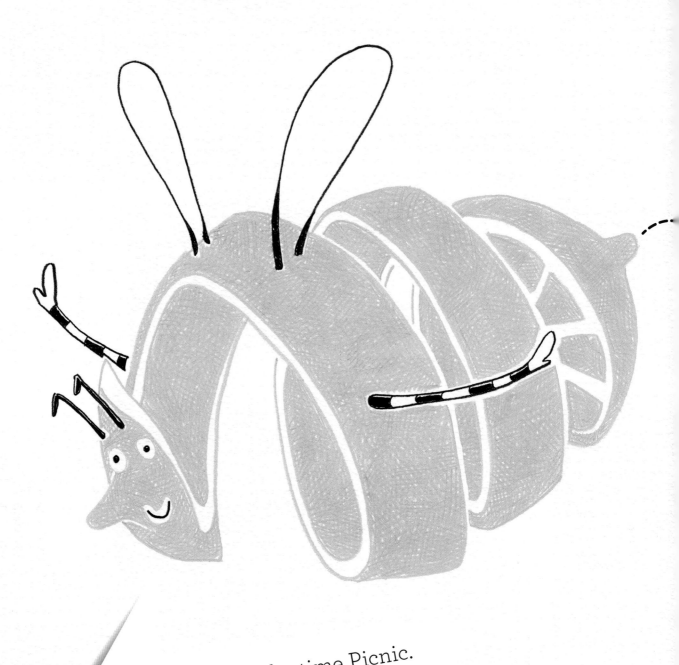

"Surprizzze, thizz iz our Playtime Picnic. Here you can have lotzz of fun with food!" says the bumblebee.

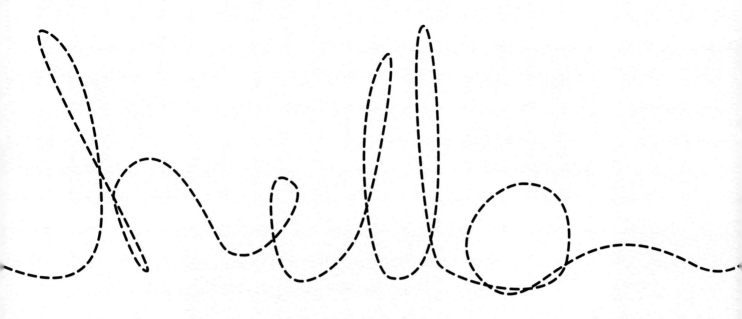

"Hello, when I meet people I must let them know, that food and I do not always go! I'm allergic to wheat, can I eat you? says Boffle.

"Well done for checking! But you're safe with me, because I am wheat and gluten-free!" buzzes the bee.

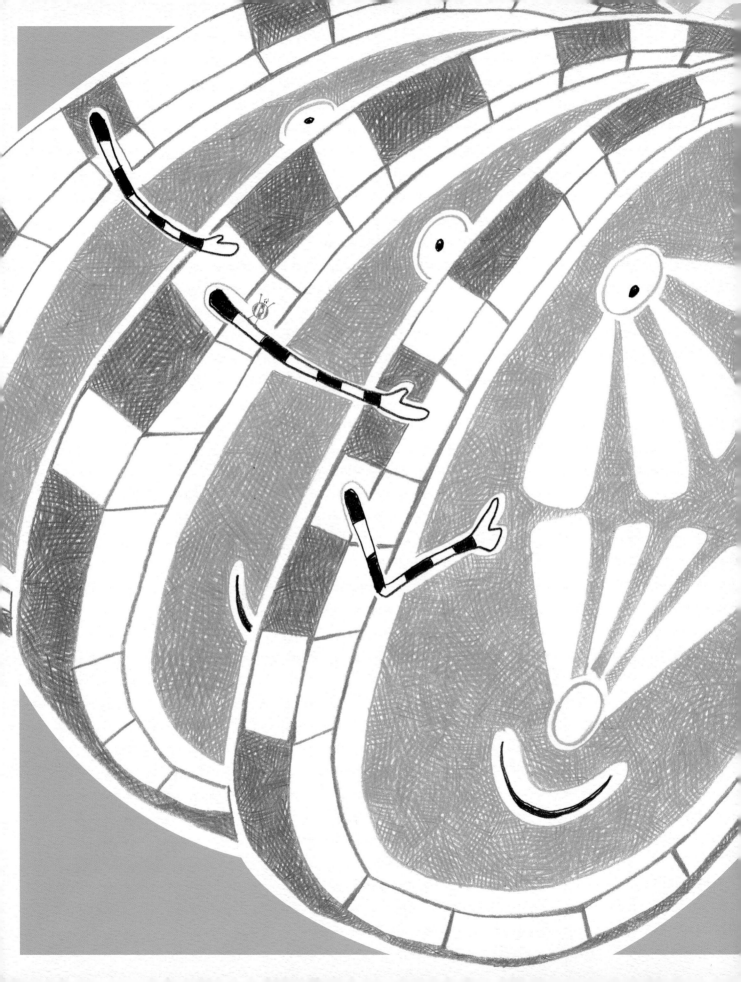

"Let'z play Frizz-bee food!"

The bee shows Boffle how to throw the cucumber slices into the wheat and gluten-free bread, like a Frisbee! If he gets them all in, he will win!

"That sounds like fun!"

1...2...3!

In this game you need a big swing,
Because all the slices have to fit in.

Boffle counts to three and shouts "Watch this!"
And with every throw he does not miss!

"Yes, you've won. It's changed from bread.
Now, it's a gluten-free sandwich instead!"

"Yippee, thank you for helping me make a tasty, wheat and gluten-free sandwich, ready for our picnic. Remember to tell everyone what food should be kept out of your tummy. So you can stay safe and have lotzzz more fun!" says the bumblebee.

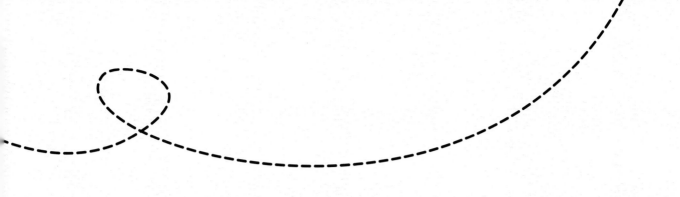

Boffle chomps on his tasty rice noodles, looking around for more games to play.

"I will! Goodbye."

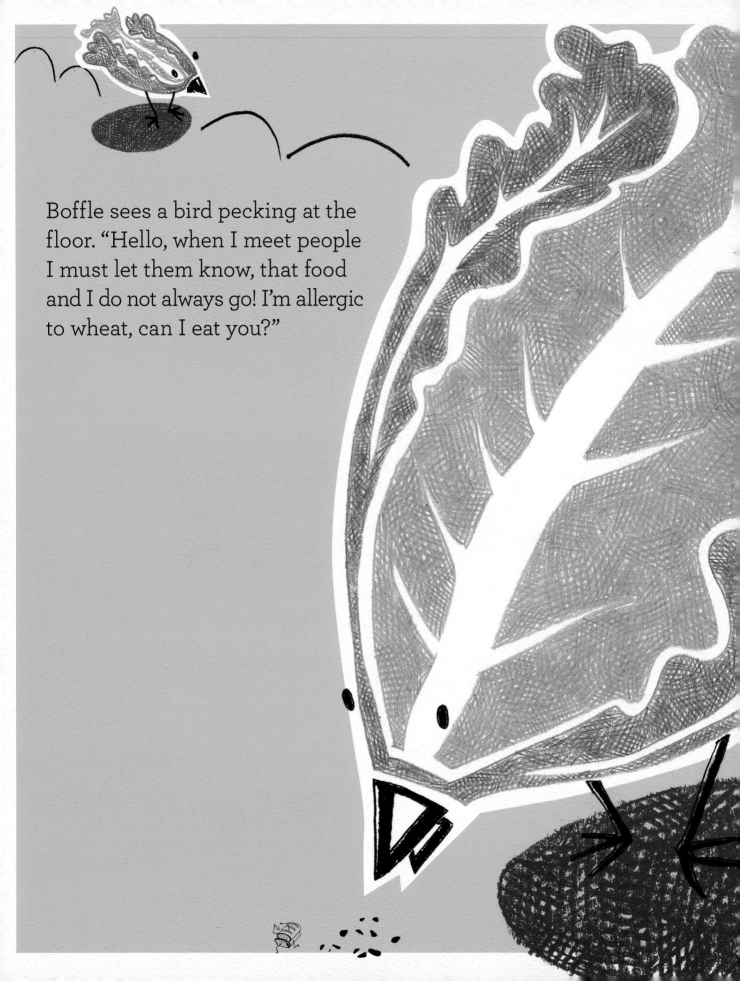

Boffle sees a bird pecking at the
floor. "Hello, when I meet people
I must let them know, that food
and I do not always go! I'm allergic
to wheat, can I eat you?"

"Got-cha!"

"Ah, hello. I'm Little Gem and you're safe with me because I am wheat and gluten-free and so is my game! Do you want to play?" asks the bird.

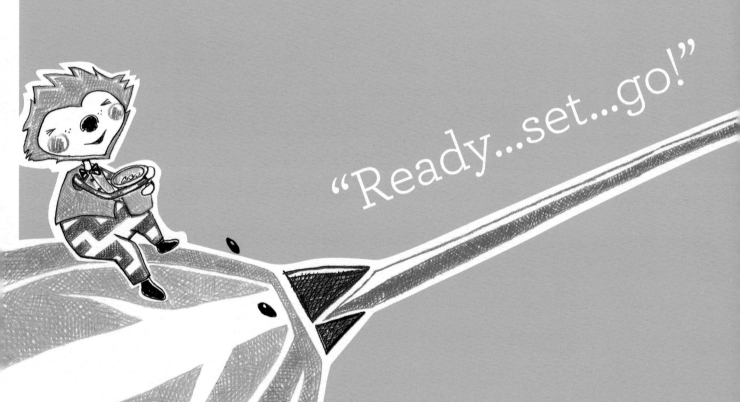

They play against Little Gem's friends from the picnic. The game begins and they all start tugging and giggling.

Boffle cheers Little Gem on to tug at the piece of grated carrot with all her might.

Can you see a face in
the bowl of vegetables?

With one big tug the bird wins, pulling her picnic friends over. "Hooray, look our bowl is now full of grated vegetables! Thank you for playing with me. I've had so much fun."

"Oh so that's why you call it Tug-of-slaw. You've made a big bowl of coleslaw!" says Boffle.

I'm dairy, soya and egg-free too!

The bird then mixes a spoonful of scrummy sauce into the bowl, to finish making coleslaw ready for the picnic.

Cake hunt!

The ants have hidden their yummy wheat and gluten-free cakes from the birds.

But now they can't remember where they've hidden them! So Boffle helps to find their cakes.

5

Can you find five cakes?

I'm wheat & gluten-free!

"Well done, you found them all before the birds ate them, hooray!" Now we know the cakes are safe, we can enjoy our picnic and have lotzz more fun!"

"Just like you on your adventure Boffle.
You told everyone about your allergy and that kept you safe, but you still had lotzz of fun too!"

"I sure did!" Boffle cheers.

"Thank you for letting me play with you all, but now it's time to go. Look! I've got one last noodle left."

"Goodbye everyone. I hope to see you again soon!"

Boffle closes his eyes and
sucks up the last noodle.
Whooshhh, it's magic!
He is back at the start.

"I love my new friends. I'm going to keep
telling everyone about my allergy, so I can
stay safe and have lots more fun!"

"When I meet people, I must let them know,
That food and I do not always go.

I repeat the words, I've been told by my mum,
To keep some foods out of my tum!

If friends follow these rules, I'll be just fine,
Having adventures all of the time!"

Meet my friends!

Sof
Fish allergy

Boskus
Peanut allergy

Didge
Milk allergy

Woot
Nut allergy

Toppi
Sesame allergy

Minoo
Egg allergy

Nessi
Soya allergy

Soon you'll be able to meet more of my allergy friends, like Boskus (who has a peanut allergy) and Nessi (who is allergic to soya). Would you like to know when their adventures are about to start? Then send an email to: new@allergyadventures.com and we'll be sure to let you know.

Whoo-hoo!

Hello, I'm Auntie H.
Two things prompted designer Hailey Phillips to create Allergy Adventures® – her diagnosis with coeliac disease and the news that an encounter with egg had sent her two-year old niece into anaphylactic shock. Watching her niece miss out on birthday cakes and other treats, Hailey wondered whether coping with food allergies could be fun and games for kids, not fear and disappointment. And so the Allergy Adventures® began...

Have your own wheat & gluten-free adventure. Make our favourite picnic platter!

Caterpillar Jackets!

Free from the top 14 allergens – Dairy, egg, nuts, peanuts, soya, fish, crustaceans, molluscs, gluten containing cereals (wheat, rye and barley), sesame, mustard, celery, lupin & sulphites.

INGREDIENTS (serves 4)

1 grown-up
4 medium potatoes
2 cloves of garlic, crushed
3 tablespoons of olive oil
Pinch of salt and pepper

METHOD

1. Take one grown-up and put them in charge!

2. Preheat your oven to 220°C. Then ask the grown up to thinly slice each potato across the middle, leaving around 1cm from the bottom intact (make sure they don't slice all the way down and take off their heads!)

3. Mix together the crushed garlic, olive oil, salt and pepper and rub the mixture all over the potatoes, even in the slits you've made. Watch out the 'caterpillars' will be really slippery and might try to escape!

4. Place the potatoes onto a baking tray and cook for about 50 minutes, until crispy on the outside but fluffy in the middle (they will fan out as they bake).

5. Take some salad leaves and make a little leafy home for your 'caterpillars' to sit on. Making them feel all snug, huddled together, ready to enjoy. Yum!

Fun activities inside this book!

Allergy adventures®
A world of serious fun

Join Boffle and his magical lunchbox as he goes on a wheat & gluten-free picnic adventure! Boffle and his friends will show you how to stay safe and have lots of fun as you find your way through the allergy maze.

Allergy Adventures® teaches children that food allergies are serious, but learning about them can be seriously good fun.

This book looks at food allergies in a different way. We don't focus on the foods to avoid and the feeling of 'missing out', we celebrate what your child can eat and explore the fun they can have with food.

And our books are not just for kids. Parents, nursery staff and friends can also use them to learn about allergies and to help promote safety around food. The books are also an excellent resource for teachers who want to explain food allergies to their class.

Allergy Adventures® has a range of books and activities to help your child understand their allergy. But just so the grown-ups don't feel left out, we've also put together some helpful insights, tips and recipes for you to enjoy! To find out more log on to allergyadventures.com

MAY CONTAIN:
We've made every story free from the top 14 allergens because children can often be diagnosed with multiple allergies. All breads, cakes, sauces, dips and creams inside this book are free from dairy, egg, nuts, peanuts, gluten-containing cereals (wheat, rye and barley), soya, fish, crustaceans, molluscs, sesame, mustard, celery, lupin & sulphites. Stories may contain allergens outside of the top 14 so if you spot one, highlight it for your child to learn and remember every time they read this book.

"Allergy Adventures® wraps up key messages in a bundle of fun and positivity."
Dr. Adam Fox
MA(Hons),MD,MSc,MB,BS,DCH,FRCPCH,FHEA,Dip. Allergy
Leading Paediatric Allergy Specialist, Guy's & St. Thomas' Hospital NHS Foundation Trust

"I want to see what happens in all of the books to meet all of the allergy friends."
Reena, Aged 4.
Ballerina & restaurant owner (when she grows up)

START ▶

Allergy adventures
A world of serious fun   allergyadventures.com

ISBN 978-1-909710-02-3
9 781909 710023

CONSCIENCE
AND **CONFLICT**

BRITISH ARTISTS AND THE
SPANISH CIVIL WAR

SIMON MARTIN